DIARY OF A
NINJA
SPY
2

Where evil goes, the ninja will follow…

*Diary of a Ninja Spy 2: The Shadow Returns
(Book 2)*

*William Thomas
Peter Patrick*

Copyright © 2016
Published by Run Happy Publishing

Chapter 1

Wow, this is unbelievable.

Really unbelievable.

If you had told me this was going to happen, I would have said, "No way! Get out! You're joking! I don't believe you!"

My name is Blake Turner, and I have been recruited by the super awesome Ninja Spy Agency to become a real ninja spy.

That's right!

A **ninja spy!**

I don't know much about ninja spies, but **ninjas** are cool and **spies** are cool, so combined they should be super cool!

Last week, I defeated the worst evil ninja that has ever existed – a guy named the Evil Shadow. The Ninja Spy Agency saw this and offered to train me further. Naturally, this top secret organization believes I have something to offer and they are willing to help me become one of the best spies in the world!

I was expecting the headquarters of the world's most amazing spy organization to be a deep underground cave on a secret tropical island, miles away from prying eyes.

But I was wrong - the headquarters are actually in my hometown.

Just three doors away from my house!

With a large neon sign!

Beats me how I never saw it before.

Tekato is my ninja mentor and he believes I have a special gift in the martial art of Ninjutsu. Today, he is going to show me around the Ninja Spy Agency HQ.

HQ is short for headquarters, not Hamburger Quest. Although I would like a hamburger.

Hmmm... hamburgers...

But I hope I get to see some cool stuff in the Ninja Spy Agency. I've been here twenty minutes already, and I haven't even been allowed in the front door yet. All I have done is fill in paperwork.

Borrring, I may as well be at school.

And I still have to go to that lame-o place too, even now that I'm going to be a spy.

Mom said if I want to be a ninja spy, I can only do it after school and on my weekends. I'm not sure if Mom understands that *evil* doesn't work to my school timetable.

"Just a few more forms to fill in, Blake," says Tekato as he hands me more paperwork.

"More? I feel like I've being here for years doing this!" I say to Tekato. "I want to do the cool stuff."

"Hmmm," Tekato sighs. "You have only filled in two forms, and now that I look at them… they don't look correct either. Blake, I know you don't live on *Butt St*, Uranus."

Ha, I'm hilarious.

"Fill it in properly, Blake. Otherwise you won't get past this desk," says Tekato. "I've taken a risk inviting you here, so don't disappoint me."

"Uhhh, fine."

I fill the form in properly so Mr. No Fun Ninja can let me in.

And filling it in properly was well worth it.

Walking into the old rundown house, I realize the inside is nothing like the outside. The inside is a state of the art, modern, secure fortress.

Wow, this place is incredible!

There are ninjas quickly darting down corridors and from room to room, all with a real purpose. They don't pay attention to me at all, which is strange because I'm the only one not dressed in a scary black outfit.

"Follow me Blake and I'll show you around. This is the heart of our global operations," Tekato tells me as we walk down the stairs to the underground section of HQ. He stops at a door, opens it, and shows me an enormous room with thousands of computers and agents working.

It is so big that the ninja spies look like little dots!

"Thousands of ninja spies are coordinated through our central control room. It is the heartbeat of everything we do. In here, we monitor every bad guy in the world. We have cameras everywhere so we can watch every move a bad guy makes."

"Including in the toilets? Because that would be weird."

"No Blake," Tekato sighs. "We do not monitor them while they use the toilet."

"And so punching bad guys is still important, right?" I ask. I don't want to sign up for a computer job – I can do that at school.

"Yes Blake, punching bad guys is still important too," replies Tekato.
As we are walking down another long corridor, a group of huge kangaroos comes charging towards us!

Tekato yanks me out of the way.

"What was that?!" I exclaim.

"They were part of an experimental ninja program. We thought that if we trained animals to help us, we could be more effective. The problem is that the NKP – the Ninja Kangaroos Program – didn't work that well and now they just bounce around the building knocking things over," answers Tekato.

"The NAP didn't work that well either."

"What was the NAP?"

"Ninja Ant Program. We sent them out to capture someone but they got distracted by a picnic nearby. We ended up with lots of sandwiches and cake, so it was good for lunch. But if you see the kangaroos coming, make sure you get out of the way."

What have I gotten myself in for....?

Chapter 2

"Blake it is time for me to show you some of the features we have here at the Ninja Spy Agency. This area here is our gadget training and experiment zone," Tekato says as he points into a room.

Standing near the entrance is a young woman in a helmet.

She is a good looking spy.

A *really* good looking spy.

Wow, she is gorgeous.

"Agent Lightning is testing our mind-reader hat," says Tekato.

Mind-reader hat! What!?

Suddenly, I look at Agent Lightning and she winks at me!

She must have read my mind!

Oh man, that is embarrassing.

Argh, now I'm going bright red! I turn away from Agent Lightning in case she notices my blushing.

"I want you to have these," Tekato hands me a pair of black leather gloves. Not much of a gift considering all the cool gadgets I can see.

The walls and tables are full of awesome looking equipment and I get a pair of gloves?

Tekato senses my disappointment. "Gloves are one of the most important tools a spy can have. All the good spies wear gloves, they hide your fingerprints. And Blake, these gloves have a few hidden abilities."

"Like what?"

"The time will come when you will need to press the buttons on your new gloves. But that time is not now."

I notice a man standing in the corner with his face to the wall.

"What's that guy doing?" I ask.

"He is watching you," says Tekato.

"No way!" I say. "He is looking at the wall."

"Throw this at him," commands Tekato as he hands me a ninja star. I haven't thrown one of these before but I launch it straight at his back.

As it is about to hit him, he moves out of its way!

"Wow, how did he see that!?"

"He is wearing rear vision glasses. They let you see what is behind you."

The ninja smiles and puts the glasses on the table. Sneaking across behind Tekato's back, I swipe them. If I fail and get kicked out of the agency today, at least I will have a few souvenirs.

"All of our ninja spies go through extensive gadget training. Our gadgets range from listening devices, smell bombs, ghost detectors, and anything else you can think of. And we have just invented the sonic Wee Bomb," Tekato leads me towards the door.

"What's a sonic Wee Bomb?" I hope it is what it sounds like.

"It is a very special type of bomb. Once you detonate it, it explodes and everyone near the bomb wets themselves."

"Ha ha! That's awesome! Can I use it?" I ask.

"No," Tekato is firm. "It is in the gadget workshop having an extra feature added."

"Can I use any of these cool spy thingamajigs?"

"We have lots of secret spy gear, but I'm not going to show you more until you complete training. Now follow me, I want to show you the dojo."

"The dojo?"

"Yes. It is where we do all of our fight training."

Ohh yeaaah, awesome.

Chapter 3

Boom!

Boom!

Boom!

The noise in the sparring room is really, really loud. Like so loud that I can barely hear myself think.

I see a giant 12-foot tall ninja battling 12 one-foot tall ninjas.

I see people being thrown in the air.

I see ninjas flipping and flying across the room.

And I see Agent Lightning staring at me.

Argh!

Think of boring non-girl thoughts!

Cabbage, cabbage, cabbage, wow she is hot.

Ekkk.

Oh, it's ok, she is not wearing the mind-reading hat now. She bows to me. I don't want to seem rude so I bow back.

Smash!

Next thing I know, I'm lying on the ground seeing stars. Agent Lightning kicked me and then walked off without an explanation!

Tekato cuts in, "In this room, if you return a bow it means you accept the challenge to a fight. Be careful who you bow in front of."

"What? I was just being polite," I grumble as I get to my feet.

"As you can see, this is where we practice our fighting skills."

"Awesome. Will you teach me how to fight like that?" I ask, pointing at a ninja who is using a hotdog as a deadly weapon.

"You will learn, but not from me," Tekato points towards a frail old man watching everyone from the middle of the room. "He will teach you."

"Him? Are you sure? He looks really old and weak. I could beat him with one arm tied behind my back while jumping on a pogo stick and eating a hamburger. The wind would probably blow him over."

Suddenly, the room falls dead silence.

Not a sound.

And everyone stares at me!

Then they all step away from the old man!
I feel like I've said something *really* stupid.

The old, weary, weak man looks mad. How
did he even hear what I said? He is 100 yards
away!

It's probably because he has massive ears.

I look at Tekato - surely he will clear this up.

But even he is distancing himself from me!

The old man walks slowly towards me.

I look down in shame, trying not to make eye contact.

"You think you can fight better than me, young man?" asks the old man with *really* stinky breath.

"No sir," I reply quietly.

He stares at me for a while and then walks back to the center of the room. With a clap, the fights begin again.

Wow, that was intense.

Chapter 4

We stand and watch the fighting for the next twenty minutes.

I quickly realize that this isn't a game for these ninja spies.

This is a serious job.

The old man claps his hands again and suddenly the room is empty.

He stares at me and says, "You will address me as Sensei."

"Yes sir," I reply in fear.

"Sensei, you stupid boy," he shouts.

Wow, he is going to be fun to train with.

Not.

I think I'd rather be at school.

"Yes, Sensei."

"Before we start any training I must know how committed you are to the ideals of the Ninja Spy Agency."

"Yeah heaps… Sensei."

"Not with words, but with actions. I want you to take these weapons to the roof and hold them above your head for as long as possible. It will show me your level of discipline."

Ahhh, seems kinda stupid.

I look at Tekato.

"We will continue the tour later. It looks like your fight training has begun," Tekato replies and then disappears out the door.

"I will have an experienced agent watch over you. They will be your guide. Do not let them down. Go, stupid boy."

Wow, this fighting guru is not a nice guy. I turn around and Agent Lightning is standing next to me with a pair of axes. She is my mentor?! Aw, man.

I take the axes and Agent Lightning leads me to the roof.

Maybe this is my chance to impress her.

"So, Agent Lightning, that's a cool name. How did you get it?" I ask as we walk onto the roof. "Can you control lightning?"

She doesn't say a word.

In fact, she has not said a word to me since we first met.

Not one word.

Maybe she can't speak?

"So... come here often?" I say to Agent Lightning.
Nothing, not a word in response.

The silent Agent Lightning leads me to the corner of the roof and motions me to lift the weapons.

I stand still, holding the weapons above my head.

Just waiting.

Man, this training is not fun. I would rather be doing my homework.

After about 20 seconds, which seems like forever, I see a lot of green smoke bellowing out of the doorway to the roof entry.

It's also bellowing out of the windows in the building.

I look to Agent Lightning, she has noticed it as well.

And she looks worried.

This isn't right.

Chapter 5

As we enter the headquarters, the smoke begins to clear.

Boring training can wait.

Sneaking around, I peep around the first corner.

The corridors are full of ninja spies lying unconscious on the ground!

And Agent Lightning looks scared!

"Is it nap time?" I joke, hoping to lighten the mood.

"No, you idiot," replies Agent Lightning. Finally, she has said something to me! Although I could have done without the insult. "Why would everyone be asleep on the ground?"

"It was a joke," I've got to be sure that she does not think I'm an idiot. "The green gas must have knocked everyone out."

"You stay here. I'm going to find out what is going on. This is no accident - the Ninja Spy Agency has been attacked," declares Agent Lightning.

Wow, she just turned it up a notch.

She went straight into mission mode.

"I'll go with you," I say, offering a hand.

"No, stay here. You are a Dumb-Dumb with no training. You will get hurt. Or worse, get me hurt."

"I'll follow. And could you please not call me a Dumb-Dumb? My name is Blake," I reply.

"Not until you prove you are not a Dumb-Dumb. You shouldn't be here, you have no talent," Agent Lightning states firmly.

I kind of preferred when she wasn't talking.

"I'm coming and I'm putting on my ninja outfit!"

"No, you are not!" snaps Agent Lightning. She pauses for a second, thinks, and continues calmly, "Yes Dumb-Dumb, put on the uniform, you can be my bait."

"Ahhhh… ok."

We move through HQ, looking into each room that we pass.

It is the same scenario over and over - all the ninja spies are out cold!

Agent Lightning and I run down a flight of stairs to see the next floor. Again, they have all been knocked out.

Every room is the same.

Hundreds of ninja spies lying on the floor.

I move ahead of Agent Lightning and rush into the control room that Tekato showed me before.

But it's the same again, everyone on the floor!

I spot movement at the far side of the room.

"Hey Lightning," I scream out. "Have a look at this!"

Agent Lightning glares at me.

"Oh no," I whisper.

Maybe I shouldn't have yelled out.

Lightning rushes in and stands beside me.

"What are you yelling about Dumb... Dumb?"

We both stare at the startled creature on the opposite side of the control room.

"Is that meant to be here?" I whisper to Lightning.

"Nuh ah," she whispers.

"Do you think it is friendly?"

"Nuh ah," she whispers again.

The giant bamboo creature walks across the large floor while never taking his eyes off us.

It's time for me to act tough and impress Agent Lightning with my bravery.

"Who are you?! Want do you want?!" I yell in my deepest voice.

"I am the Bamboo Dragon!" it yells back.

"What do you want?!" I keep yelling.

"I…want…your…lives!"

Uh-oh…This dude looks angry…

Chapter 6

The Bamboo Dragon shoots a blast towards us!

We both dive out of the way!

Whoa – that was close.

I sneak behind a computer desk but I can hear Agent Lightning and the Bamboo Dragon fighting each other. I look up and I see that Agent Lightning is in trouble. The Bamboo Dragon has her pinned against the wall trying to punch her.

I need to do something!

Now!

I bring out the axes that I have been training with and leap onto a table.

"Hey Bamboo Dragon!" I yell.

He turns towards me.

"You suck!" I yell.

Yep, that clearly wasn't the best thing I could have yelled.

"No, you suck," the Bamboo Dragon replies.

"You suck more!" I yell again.

I pull out my ninja mask and slip it on.

Action time!

I jump from table to table towards the Bamboo Dragon.

I am able to chop at its arms with my axes - but the Bamboo Dragon slaps me across the room!

Agent Lightning leaps at the giant moving tree, and she is slapped aside as well!

This dude is tough!

While she is recovering on the floor, I make another charge at the Bamboo Dragon.

Another unsuccessful attack!

But as I am about to run away, it grabs hold of me!
I take a hit in the back.

It's not fun being punched from behind.

I grab the rear vision glasses I 'borrowed' from the experiment lab and put them on. Now I can see everything that is happening behind me.

Every punch the Bamboo Dragon throws at me, I am able to dodge even though I'm facing the wrong way.

Awesome!

Meanwhile, I can see Agent Lightning climbing to her feet. She jumps up and karate chops the Bamboo Dragon's arm and it falls off!

"My arm! My beautiful bamboo arm!"

"What are you doing here, Stick Man?!" demands Agent Lightning.

"I am here to destroy the Ninja Spy Agency!"

"Why? Who are you working for?" Agent Lightning yells.

But I want to ask some questions too.

"What are your favorite board-games?" I yell.

The Bamboo Dragon repeats itself, "I am here to destroy the Ninja Spy Agency!"

"We won't be able to defeat this guy unless we attack together," I say to Agent Lightning.

"Ahhhh. You are right. Let's do this," Agent Lightning agrees.

We both attack.

I leap up, jumping on his back, and I see a loose wire. I grab at it and yank it out.

"He was a robot!" I yell.

The giant robot falls to the ground lifeless.

I did it!

I saved the day!

Cool!

"Nice work, Dumb-Dumb," says Agent Lightning.

Wow, it is hard to get respect around here.

"There is a name tag on the robot," I say as I lean down. "Property of… oh no… the **Evil Shadow**!"

Chapter 7

"Who is the Evil Shadow?" asks Agent Lightning.

"The Evil Shadow is your most dangerous nemesis. He has vowed to destroy the Ninja Spy Agency!" I continue, "He must have sent the robot to gather vital information about the Ninja Spy Agency from the control room."

"Ohhh, that Evil Shadow. Right, I know the one," Agent Lightning says. "I usually work on small time thieves, not the big bosses."

"Well, I've meet this goon before. He is a few hundred years old and is cursed to destroy the Ninja Spy Agency. He is really dangerous. He had been destroying landmarks around the world for fun. And he really hates everything. Like everything. Even pizza! But I own a magical sword that can defeat him," I explain to Agent Lightning.

I'm really showing my strengths now!

"Where is the sword?" asks Lightning.

"Uh, I lost it somewhere. I'm not very tidy and I misplace things a lot," I respond with disappointment.

"Well, if this is his robot, he must be behind this intrusion. He will be held responsible for the gassing of our agents!"

Suddenly a loud voice remarks from the door, "You will never hold me responsible, little agent!"

It is the Evil Shadow!

He is back! And I don't have my sword this time!

"Not you again," I say.

"How did you find us? Nobody knows our secret location!" asks Agent Lightning.

"You foolish spies, you lead me straight to your HQ! I simply followed Blake around until you brought him in for training," the Evil Shadow states.

Agent Lightning gives me a dirty look as if to say this is my fault – but I'm not the one who led him here, that was Tekato!

Agent Lightning doesn't bother to talk anymore.

She charges full pace at the Evil Shadow.
A straight up assault on him!

The Evil Shadow lifts his hands slowly and flicks a small piece of dust at Lightning. Instantly Agent Lightning starts sneezing uncontrollably.

AH-CHOO! AH-CHOO! AH-CHOO! AH-CHOO! AH-CHOO! AH-CHOO! AH-CHOO!

Wow, that looks like it is starting to hurt.

AH-CHOO!

"Dumb-Dumb help! Make it stop!" she sneezes out.

"Calling me Dumb-Dumb is not going to get my help," I reply.

"Ha ha," laughs the Evil Shadow. "Are you lovers having relationship trouble?"

"We, AH-CHOO! are, AH-CHOO! NOT, AH-CHOO! LOVERS! AH-CHOO!" declares Lightning. Wow, she didn't have to scream it. Surely she could do worse than me.

"AH-CHOO! Do something!" begs Agent Lightning. "You cannot let him win! We must stop him! The world is at risk!"

I was attracted to Agent Lightning up until this point. But now she is covered from head to toe in snot, I'm having second thoughts.

AH-CHOO! AH-CHOO! AH-CHOO! AH-CHOO!

Yuck. Seriously, there is so much snot, it is gross!

And she still keeps calling *me* Dumb-Dumb.

"Your move now, Blake," the Evil Shadow shouts.

At least he uses my name.

"Bring it on!" I say as I slip on my ninja spy gloves.

Chapter 8

I dart across the room and make my way towards the Evil Shadow.

Hopefully my attack will work out better than Agent Lightning's attempt!

With a few yards to go, I increase my speed. My plan is simple - run into him at a high speed. No arty ninja dancing, just a big, plain old bump.

I press a button on the ninja gloves that says 'Hammer.' I don't know what it does, but I'll give anything a go.

Suddenly a hammer head appears in place of my right glove!

Awesome!

As I strike at the Evil Shadow, he darts to the side and the hammer hand smashes straight into the wall.

I pull it out and press another button on my gloves - this one is labelled "Laser". I hope this one is a powerful laser that cuts through my opponent!

Nope.

Damn.

I was wrong about the laser button - it is a button for a disco strobe light.

Great for entertaining but not great for battling the world's meanest guy.

But I make the most of the situation and dance my way to the Evil Shadow.

Maybe we can have a dance-off to settle this?

I smirk at him. He smiles back and then moves into an attacking stance. The dance-off looks like it is not going to happen today. Maybe another day.

The Evil Shadow grabs me and easily throws me through a wall into another room.

Ouch. That hurt.

But I have landed in the spy gadget room!

Awesome!

I can see the mind-reader hat that Agent Lightning was using earlier! I put it on and run back towards the Evil Shadow through the hole in the wall.

"What is that ridiculous looking helmet doing on your head?" asks the Evil Shadow.

"Hey! What do you know about fashion? This is the latest trend, all the cool ninjas are wearing it," I lie to him to cover up my brilliant secret weapon!

Every move he makes, I'll be able to counter it using the mind-reader.

The Evil Shadow throws a left-hand punch and I easily counter it with a right-hand block.

I knew that was coming.

The Evil Shadow looks stunned.

He delivers a kick towards my chest, but I knew he was going to do that, so I move back a step!

Reading his mind again, I can tell that he is frustrated.

I don't even have to be good at fighting now! This invention could save me from completing all the vigorous training.

I read his mind again - he is thinking about a three punch combo!

He delivers but again, I am able to counter it.

Now he is thinking about… dinner?

He wants tacos for dinner. Wow, he is not focusing at all!

I turn my body and set myself up for my final kick-butt finishing move.

A quick scan of his thoughts and I know I've timed my move perfectly. As he lifts his guard, I strike at his chest.

THUMP! THUMP! THUMP!

I'm on the ground?! What?! How?! Something hit me hard and I didn't see it coming!

As my eyes focus, I realize that it wasn't the Evil Shadow that outsmarted me.

It was the mob of wild kangaroos roaming the building!

They just bounced straight through me.

Worse still, they crushed my mind-reading helmet!

As I get to my feet, I realize that the Evil Shadow has disappeared.

Oh no.

This is not good.

I run over to Agent Lightning, "Are you ok? Where did he go?"

"I'm fine now, I've sneezed all the snot out of me," she replies.

Eww.

"The Evil Shadow ran into that office," Agent Lightning continues.

Together we bust in on the Evil Shadow in the next room – ready to fight!

But he isn't fighting.

He is going through our files. That's odd.

"What are you looking for?" I ask.

"The password!"

"The password for what?"

"For your computer system! Once I'm in the mainframe, I can shut down all the Ninja Spy Agency programs! Ha ha ha!"

He really does have an evil laugh.

"Ah ha! Here it is! The password!" rejoices the Evil Shadow as he reaches for the desk lamp.

"*The-evil-shadow-is-stupid*? That's not a very nice password," he continues.

"Why did you leave the password on a sticky note attached to a lamp?" I ask Agent Lightning, "That doesn't seem very secure."

"Well, that was not my idea," answers Agent Lightning.

"Victory is mine at last!" the Evil Shadow declares.

Chapter 9

Agent Lightning and I chase the Evil Shadow back to the control room.

"You can't stop me, Blake! I've got enough information to break into your top secret computer files and corrupt your entire network!"

"Don't you dare!" yells Agent Lightning.

I lean across to Lightning, "I have an idea. Keep him in the room until I give the signal. Watch this."

I press a button on my spy gloves and my finger turns into a screwdriver.

I find the fuse box on the wall that powers the control room. I undo some screws and the power to the room goes out!

He can't corrupt the system if it is not on!

I've done it!

I stopped him!

"Hey! Where is the power?! Turn that back on!" cries the Evil Shadow.

"Lightning! Run towards the window!"

Agent Lightning runs for the window as I enter the control room with my secret weapon - the Wee Bomb!

Yes!

I get a chance to use it!

I throw the Wee Bomb to the Evil Shadow and he catches it!

Ha ha, sucker!

"What was that?" asks Agent Lightning.

"The Wee Bomb – and it's set to level MAXIMUM WEE! We need to get out of here ASAP! This is going to get ugly!"

I grab Agent Lightning, push open the window, and jump out.

"Aargh!" screams Lightning, "What are you doing?!"

As we are falling towards the ground, I hit the buttons on my gloves and parachutes come out from my hands!

Behind us there is a loud, *squishy* explosion!

Boom!

Splat!

Yuck! Yuck. Yucky yuck.

While we are gliding to safety, I can hear the Evil Ninja crying in embarrassment!

Epilogue

Later that day...

The Evil Ninja is now in the Ninja Spy Agency jail.

Apparently that's impossible to break out of.

As the ninja spies wake up from the sleeping gas, they all seem a little shocked that I have saved the day. I don't think they believe it, but luckily Agent Lightning is around to tell them what happened.

"Well done, Blake! You did it!" says Tekato. "But did you really need to detonate the Wee Bomb inside? This will take weeks to clean up."

"At least now we can smell if the Evil Shadow is coming," I reply.

Tekato continues, "If you are interested, we have an assignment for you, Blake. We have been investigating the disappearance of our sacred spell books and -"

"Sure," I interrupt, "I'd love to help. But I really need to get to school this week. So if you haven't solved it by Saturday, then I'll do it!"

"Hmmm…" Tekato thinks. "Yes, school is important. We'll see you on Saturday."

Oh yeah.

Another ninja weekend coming up!

The End